90-1028

j910
COO

Cooper, Kay

Where in the world are you?

$14.85

DATE		
OV 24 1990		
EC 3 1990		
NOV 19 1991		
JUN 2 1 1993		
JUL 16 1993		
JAN 1 7 1995		
DEC 0 3 2008		

© THE BAKER & TAYLOR CO.

WHERE IN THE WORLD ARE YOU?

A Guide to Looking at the World

WHERE IN THE WORLD ARE YOU?

A Guide to Looking at the World

by Kay Cooper

Illustrations by Justin Novak

Walker and Company
New York

First published in the United States of America in 1990
by Walker Publishing Company, Inc.

Published simultaneously in Canada by Thomas Allen & Son
Canada, Limited, Markham, Ontario

Library of Congress Cataloging-in-Publication Data

Cooper, Kay.
Where in the world are you? / by Kay Cooper; illustrations by
Justin Novak.
Summary: Discusses the field of geography and how it helps you locate
where you are or where you might like to be.
ISBN 0-8027-6912-8.—ISBN 0-8027-6913-6 (lib. bdg.)
1. Geography—Miscellanea—Juvenile literature. [1. Geography.]
I. Novak, Justin, ill.   II. Title.
G133.C66   1990 910—dc20   89-27444

Printed in the United States of America

2   4   6   8   10   9   7   5   3   1

90-1028

TO MY BEST FRIEND, PATRICIA A. MIZEUR

TABLE OF CONTENTS

WHERE IN THE WORLD ARE YOU?

A Guide to Looking at the World

★ 1 ★

CLUES TO WHERE YOU ARE

Where in the world are you? Are you somewhere in a city? In the middle of a storm? Near your favorite pizza restaurant?

Wherever you are is a place. And that place is part of geography.

Geography is the study of places, why they are there, and what kinds of people, plants, animals, minerals, climates, and land and water areas make up these places.

A geographer can be an expert on a very large place—such as the state of Alaska—or use satellites to map the entire world. A geographer also can be an expert on a small place, such as a mountain range or even a small town. In fact, a geographer can study almost any place and call it geography.

You use geography when you go from place to place—out the front door, down the street, and to a neighbor's house. Geography helps you find places and explain where these places are located. For example, if you hear on the radio today that a new restaurant will be giving away free pizza next Saturday afternoon at Second and Washington, you'll probably want to go. But where is Second and Washington? How do you find it? If you aren't there Saturday, you're out of luck. Since you don't know where Second and Washington is, you might ask a friend for directions. Your friend might say:

"Well, you go down Main Street past a sign that says WORMS FOR SALE, then you turn left. Or is it right? I think it's left. Well anyway, there's a pink house on the corner. And you can't miss a pink house. So you turn there and go to Billy's house. Then you go about five or six blocks until you come to some big trees and it's about four or five blocks beyond the trees."

Do you think you'll ever find the pizza place by following this person's directions?

The best way to find the pizza restaurant is to ask someone who can give you such good directions that your mind can picture exactly where the pizza place is. This picture is your own mental map and it will lead you from the place where you are to the restaurant.

Surprisingly enough, you already have countless mental maps inside your head. These maps lead you from your bed to the bathroom at night and from any place in your home to the TV set. You use mental maps when you walk around your neighborhood or when you go in and out of rooms in your home and school.

If a route to the pizza restaurant—or any other place—is too complicated, however, you'll need a map to get there. A *map* is a drawing or picture showing all you need to know to get to the place you want to go.

Most maps are drawn with north at the top, so it's important that you always know where you are in relation to north. Do you know, for example, which side of your home faces north? Which side of your school?

Just For Fun

To find north, get up early one morning and watch the sun rise. It rises in the east. If your home has windows that face east, the morning sun will shine through them. If you are facing the rising sun, north will be on your left.

On most maps, north is at the top, east is on the right, south is at the bottom, and west is on the left. These four directions—north, east, south, and west— are called the *cardinal directions*. They are the most important directions shown on a map.

The directions halfway between the cardinal directions are called the *intermediate* or *in-between direc-*

tions. They are named by putting the names of two cardinal directions together. For example, the intermediate direction between north and east is called northeast. The others are: southeast, southwest, and northwest.

But do you always remember which direction is west and which direction is east? Many people have trouble determining east and west as well as left and right. Perhaps you are like a girl who writes "left" and "right" on the backs of her hands in order to take piano lessons.

If you don't like to think about "left" and "right," create games that you do like in order to remember left and right. Wear a ring only on your right hand and tell yourself that the "r" in ring stands for the "r" in right. You could avoid "left" and "right" words and say, "That way to Liz" and "That way to Robin." But this only works if you tell people that Liz stands for "left" and Robin stands for "right"!

If you have trouble remembering the cardinal directions, create an acronym, a word formed by the first letters of a series of words. For example, "Never eat soggy waffles" is an acronym for north, east, south, and west. Think, too, that if N(orth) is at the top of your map, then W(est) and E(ast) say "WE" across the middle of your map. What other acronyms can you create to help you always remember the cardinal directions?

Knowing the cardinal and intermediate directions will help you find your way to the places you want to go. They also will help you tell someone else where the pizza place is. You might say:

"Go north on Main Street until you reach Tomato Street. Turn right at Tomato and go five blocks east to Cheese Street. The pizza restaurant is on the southwest corner of Tomato and Cheese streets."

★ 2 ★

There's No Place Like Home

Would you like to go to the largest amusement park in the world, track down Pinocchio, and see the castle shown in the movie, "Chitty-Chitty-Bang-Bang"?

How can you find your way to these places if you don't know where they are? To find your way around, it's best to start from the one place you know better than anywhere else in the world—your own home.

To do this, you'll need pencils with good erasers, a large piece of paper, a map of your city, and a road or highway map showing your state. Your parents may have these maps, and there may be a city map pictured in your telephone book. Gas stations, visitor centers, local bookstores, and public and school libraries will have the maps you need, too.

Just For Fun

Draw a very tiny box for your house or apartment in the middle of a large piece of paper. Label the side of your home that faces the rising sun "east." Write in the other cardinal directions—north, south, west—around your home. Make the side you marked "north" the top of your map.

Is there a driveway, street, sidewalk, wall, or fence around your house or apartment? These *man-made features* may be boundaries around your home. Other boundaries may be *natural features*, such as a river, lake, field, ocean, forest, or swamp. If you aren't certain what borders your home, ask your parents what the boundaries are. Perhaps the bushes planted between your house and the neighbor's mark a boundary line.

On your map, make little drawings of the trees, streets, and other features that border your home.

Your City or Town

If you're a good enough detective, you'll be able to find the very spot on the city map where your home is. Remember, you already know how your home lines up with the direction north. So, look for the cardinal directions on the city map.

Perhaps your map includes a list of all the streets in your town. This list is in alphabetical order. All you have to do is to find the name of your street in the list. After its name is a letter and number. The letter and number will help you find your street. Letters mark the lines running across the map. Numbers mark the lines running up and down the map. These lines are equally spaced. They cross one another and are called *grid lines*.

Let's say that your street's letter and number is C-18. Drawn an imaginary line from the letter C and from the number 18. Where these lines cross on the map is a *grid square* containing your street.

Now, notice the general shape of your city. Does it resemble a lot of squares put together? Or is it some strange shape? Whatever it is, draw a very small outline the same shape as your city around your home. Make sure your home is located in the right spot. If you live on the north side, for example, draw your city so that your home is located on the north side. Don't worry about drawing the lines of your city perfectly. A rough outline will do. Inside the drawing, write your city's name.

Your County

Can you draw your county around your city? If you live in Alaska, you'll probably draw your borough; and you'll draw your parish if you live in Louisiana. If you live in the national capital, Washington, D.C., you are in a unique situation. You don't live in a county or a state. You live in the city of Washington which covers an area called "D.C.," meaning the "District of Columbia." In Washington, D.C., "city" and "district" have the same meaning.

To see what your county looks like, look at a road or highway map showing your state. Along one side of this map is an index listing the names of the counties in alphabetical order. Find the name of your county in the index and locate the grid square containing your county.

You'll probably notice that the name of your county and its boundaries are in the same color. Trace the boundaries of your county with your finger to learn its general shape. Then draw a rough sketch of your county around your city and label it.

What borders your county? Find out by looking again at the road map. Draw the other counties and the natural features that border your county. Label them by their names.

Your State

Does your state have an interesting shape? Oklahoma is shaped like a cooking pot, with a long handle pointing west. Maine resembles a buffalo head; Colorado is a perfect rectangle; and the lower part of Michigan looks like a mitten.

When you decide what your state resembles, sketch this shape around the counties you've drawn. At the bottom of your map, write your state's name and add what you think your state resembles. You might write, "California. My state looks like my arm."

Which states and natural features border your state? Perhaps another country—Canada or Mexico—forms a boundary. Write the names of all the northern boundaries in the area north of your state. Continue to add boundary names for those places east, south, and west.

If you live in Missouri or Tennessee, you'll discover that your state is surrounded by eight other states. If you live in Utah, Colorado, Arizona, or New Mexico, you'll discover a place where you can stand in your state and three other states all at once—that is, if you have four legs. It's the only place in the United States where corners of four states meet. Alaska and Hawaii are the only states that don't touch any other state. And Maine only touches one—New Hampshire.

A few states, such as Colorado, do not have any boundaries formed by water. Hawaii, however, is our only island state and is completely surrounded by water—the Pacific Ocean. Natural water boundaries— oceans, lakes, and rivers—look crooked or wavy on a map. Find the natural water boundaries that form your state's boundaries. Add these names to the appropriate places on your map.

Check a United States map to discover if your state is smaller or larger than the states surrounding it. If your state were to be placed over a surrounding state, would there be some areas not covered? The state of Vermont, for example, could be placed over New York and much of New York would not be covered. You can see that New York is much larger than Vermont.

Add your state's size to your map. If you live in Alaska, you can write, "My state is the largest in the United States." If your home state is Rhode Island, you'll probably write, "My state is the smallest in the United States." If you live in Georgia, you can write, "My state is the largest state east of the Mississippi River."

Cities in Your State

How many people live in your hometown? Cities are shown by dots on a map. The size and design of a dot or the size of the town's name will give you a clue about the population of a city. Large dots on the map show cities with large populations; small dots show smaller populations. A town's name set in large type shows a large population, and small type indicates a smaller population.

Is your state capital the largest city in your state? The capital is shown by a star in a circle. Sometimes the capital isn't the largest city. None of the three largest cities in the United States—New York, Los Angeles, and Chicago—is a state capital.

Just For Fun

Draw a star where your state capital is and write its name on your map. Is your town larger or smaller than the capital? Add this information to your map by drawing a large or small dot to show your city's size.

You also can add your county seat to your map. County seats are cities where county government offices are located. They may be shown by a dot of a certain design. Find your county seat and create your own dot design for it. Write the name of the county seat by your dot.

Your map is now a picture of where you live.

Creating Symbols for Your Map

People will understand your map better if you create *symbols* for the places and features you want to show. You already have some symbols on your map: the dots for cities, the star in a circle for your state capital, and the tiny box for your home.

Map symbols may be colors, too. Colors on a map usually tell something about the natural features of a place. Blue is often used to show water. Greens and browns are used to show *land elevations,* or the height of land above the surface of the ocean after all the wave motions have been smoothed out. Sometimes, land elevations are shown by a number that tells how many feet a place is above *sea level*.

A map's *legend* or *key* explains its symbols. A road map's legend, for example, shows symbols for highways, airports, campgrounds, and much more. Some legends on road maps even show railroad passenger routes through the state.

You can create your own legend by listing all the places you want to show on your map. List these places on a separate piece of paper. You might want to list your county and state boundaries, lakes, mountains, and rivers. After each item on your list, put a little drawing or a color. The drawings and colors are your symbols. Draw these symbols on your map. Tape or staple your legend to your map.

What Is Your Hometown Like?

Do you know what makes your hometown different from the other places you've been? Does it have the tallest, the biggest, the only, or the most of anything? Does it have a historic site where an important event in history happened? Is a product such as tennis shoes, jet planes, or computers manufactured there?

Do crops such as corn, potatoes, or oranges grow there? Where do the people of your town work—in factories, farms, or mines? Is your town noisy, smelly, smoggy, or dirty? What's the weather like? Is your town located in the mountains, desert, or along a seashore or riverbank? What do you like and dislike about your town? If a visitor came to your town, what would you show him?

Names—Do you live in Fairview, Midway, Oak Grove, Riverside, or Centerville? These are the most popular city names in the United States. There are Fairviews—the number one name—in 31 states. Many Fairviews were named because the name matched the location. An early settler of Fairview, Oklahoma, hiked a hill overlooking the town's future site and declared, "That's a fair view." And from Fairview, Pennsylvania, the fair view is Lake Erie.

If your town's name doesn't match its location, perhaps its nickname does. One of San Francisco's nicknames is "Bay City." And "City of Good Living" is the nickname for Anaheim, California, where Disneyland is located.

Many names and nicknames are descriptive. Quartzsite, Arizona, is known as "The Hottest Town" because its average July temperature is 108.7 degrees Fahrenheit.

Other names tell something about the town's history. Ballena, a village in San Diego County, California, was given its name because a whale once was stranded on the beach. *Ballena* is the Spanish word

24

for "whale." A valley and a mountain shaped like a whale also are named "Ballena" in San Diego County.

If your town's name or nickname matches its location, describes it, or tells something about its history, add this information to your map.

Streets—Look at your city map to see if you can solve some mysteries about the way your city's streets are numbered. Do you see any streets changing their names when they cross a particular street? Does West Sandwich suddenly become East Sandwich? If you can find all the streets changing their names as they cross the same street, then you've found one of the most important streets in your town. This street is known as zero street because all the street numbers become higher along the streets running in either direction away from zero street.

One zero street usually leads to another zero street. This zero is the second place where streets change their names. North Duckwater becomes South Duckwater. Where the two zero streets come together is your city's zero point. This is the place with the lowest street numbers in town. Once you know where zero point is, you'll be able to tell where 1300 West Vampire is, even though you have never heard of it.

If your address is a low number, you either live downtown—where the lowest numbers usually are found—or on a street that isn't included in your city's numbering system. Such a street may be far from downtown. Add your address and how far you live from the downtown area to your map.

Land Elevation—How high is your town above the

surface of the ocean? To find out, look at a *physical map* that shows the natural features of your state. Your school and public libraries will have the map you need. Also find out the highest and lowest elevations in your state. This information is printed on your state road map next to a colored square that is the symbol for "point of interest."

Here is how you can add land elevations to your map:

1. Draw a ring around the highest elevation in your state and color it dark brown. Write how high it is and the name of the place on your map.
2. Circle your state's lowest elevation and color it dark green. Add the height and the place's name.
3. Select a color to show your town's elevation. A shade of green will show that the elevation is near the lowest. A brown shade will show that it's near the highest.

Do you think that elevation makes a difference in peoples' lives, occupations, agriculture, and the weather?

If you guess that the higher the elevation the lower the temperature, you are right. A hike up a mountain can be a journey from hot temperatures to freezing ones. The temperature will fall about 3 to 5.5 degrees Fahrenheit every 1,000 feet you climb. On your hike you might notice that one side of the mountain valley is in sunshine, while the other side is in the mountain's shadow. Orchards grow and dairy cows graze on the mountain slope. Near the top of the mountain is a ski resort and a forest of evergreen trees. If you climb high enough, you'll reach the snow line where snow covers the ground even on the hottest summer days.

Can you think how your town's elevation affects you and other people living there? If you know, add words and symbols to show these effects. For example, if you live in the corn belt, which stretches from Nebraska to Illinois, you might draw an ear of corn, a sun, and raindrops. You might also add an elevation color to show flatland. These symbols all mean that your area has the right weather and land for growing corn.

What Is Your State Like?

What do you know about your state? If you don't know much about it, you will want to do some research in the library to learn what makes your state special. Does it have the highest, lowest, biggest, most, or only of anything? Was a president or vice president of the United States born in your state? Does your state produce minerals, such as coal or copper? Or does it produce a fuel, such as petroleum or natural gas?

In the process of searching for facts about your state, look for information that relates to your hometown. The nickname given to your state, for example, could describe your town. Ohio, for instance, is the Buckeye State. If you live in this state and a buckeye tree grows in your yard or is one of the main trees growing in your town, then draw a buckeye tree, leaf, or nut on your map. Here are some more ideas about what you can add:

27

Names—Do you know how your state was named? About half of the states have names of Indian origin. Most of the others were named for places or people. Does the French word "vermont," meaning "green mountains," describe your hometown? If it does and you live in Vermont, add the meaning of this word to your map.

State Symbols—Do you ever see your state's bird, flower, insect, mineral, tree, animal, or fish in your hometown? If you do, add them to your map. Each state has its symbols to tell something important about it. Many times, school children of a state helped choose the symbols. Some states even have a state dance, gem, beverage, and grass.

Most states have special brochures explaining all of their symbols. You can obtain a copy by writing to the secretary of state in your capital city.

Geographical Center—Where's the *geographical center* of your state? The geographical center is that part on which the surface of your state would balance if the entire state were the same thickness. The geographical center of the United States, including Alaska and Hawaii, is Butte County, South Dakota, just west of Castle Rock. The geographical center for the contiguous United States, which includes the 48 states plus the District of Columbia, is near Lebanon, Kansas. The word *"contiguous"* means "touching one another."

Reference books such as a world almanac will tell you where the geographical center of your state is. Add this information to your map.

Now that you've finally finished your map, you can see where your home really is. As a result, you will have a good idea how it compares to the other places you'll be visiting in this book.

⋆ 3 ⋆

WHERE ARE YOUR RELATIVES
AND FRIENDS?

Do you have a relative or friend living in another state or country? Have you ever gone there for a visit? How far was it? How did you know which way to go? You probably didn't, but the person who took you looked at a map which showed how far you had to go and in which direction.

If you traveled by car, you saw the driver using a road or highway map. This map shows where towns and cities are located. It also shows what roads lead to each town and what directions to travel.

The colored lines on the map are the main highways. Some highways are marked by tiny squares. These square symbols show where you can drive off and on these highways. The number of the highway also is shown on the map. The shape of the symbol around the highway number tells if it is an Interstate Highway (shown by a shield), a State Highway (shown by an oval or circle), or a United States Route (also shown by a shield).

Interstate highways are long roads that connect the largest cities in the United States. Interstate 80, for example, goes from San Francisco on the Pacific coast to the George Washington Toll Bridge, which crosses the Hudson River into New York City. You can cover distances quicker on interstates because there aren't any traffic lights. Interstates can handle heavy vehicles, such as large trucks and military tanks.

U.S. highways connect large cities and small towns, while state highways connect cities and towns with the interstates and U.S. highways. Some state highways connect small towns to each other. You'll probably notice that some roads do not have numbers. These are rural roads shown by a particular color, usually black or gray.

Just For Fun

Let's suppose that you are going to travel by car to a relative's home in another state. Look at the road map and see how far it is from your home to your relative's home. Miles usually are shown between arrows (red map symbols). On the map you will see which highways to take and which rivers and mountains to cross.

With your finger, follow the route you'll be taking from your home to your relative's. Along the route, look for map symbols. Check the map's legend to discover what these symbols mean. You may discover that the route takes you past a state park, ski area, dam, national park, and a famous golf course.

Make a list of the places you'd like to see along the way. Select one or two places, and then ask the person who'll be driving if he or she would stop at the places you'd like to visit.

Does your relative or friend live in a large city? Your school and local public libraries will have travel guides, histories, and maps of large cities. Information on small towns is often included in travel guides, too. Read about the city you'll be visiting and select one thing you'd like to do there. Then do it!

Pathways To Fun

Do you ever wish you had something to guide you to unfamiliar places so you'd never become lost? Try *orienting*. What's orienting? It's placing a map so that the directions on the map are the same as the directions on the ground. If a road map shows your relative's home is 100 miles north and 400 miles west, you must travel north and west on the ground.

The best way to orient a map is to place it next to a direction-finding instrument called a *compass*. A compass needle, which turns on a pivot, points north. Place the map so that north on the map points in the same direction as the needle. Now the cardinal directions are the same on the compass and on the map.

Orienting has a lot to do with orienteering—a popular sport in Sweden and Norway. Orienteering is a cross-country race in which competitors use a map and compass to find a pathway that someone else has laid out through a forest. Along the path are colored flags which mark checkpoints. The first person to reach the finish line having touched all the flags wins.

Getting oriented to the woods with a compass and map is becoming popular in the New England states, Missouri, California, and Washington. You can find out more about orienteering by writing Orienteering Services, USA, P.O. Box 1604, Binghampton, New York 13902.

Different Countries and the Globe

Do you have a relative or friend living in another country? Did someone in your family serve in the armed forces overseas? From which countries did your ancestors come? If you don't know the answers to these questions, ask your parents or another relative.

Once you know the names of the countries that mean something to your family, make a list and locate them on a world map or globe. But how can you find a country when you don't have the faintest idea where to start looking for it? You can find it if you have a good reference book, such as a book of maps, an encyclopedia, or a geographical dictionary. Look up the country's name in the book's table of contents or index, or find the country's name in the alphabetical list of places listed in the dictionary. Your teacher or a librarian also can help you find sources to locate the country.

Once you know where the country is, locate it on a *globe*. A globe is the best map to use because it gives you the best idea of distance, direction, and the shapes and sizes of land and water areas. This is because a globe is the same shape as the earth—a ball.

On a globe, the location which is the farthest point north is the North Pole. If you lived there the windows on all four sides of your house would face south. You wouldn't be living on land, but rather on a frozen ocean surrounded by land.

The point farthest south on the globe is the South Pole. Here all the windows in your house would face north. The United States has a scientific station at the South Pole to solve such mysteries as how this frozen land affects the world's weather.

When you look at a globe, you can see lines drawn on it. Mapmakers drew these lines to help you locate places on the earth. The lines going around the globe are lines of *latitude*. Because they are parallel lines, they also are called *parallels*. Each line is a complete circle around the globe. The longest line is the *equator*, which is halfway between the North and South Poles.

Latitude lines are numbered from 0 degrees at the equator to 90 degrees north and south. The North Pole is 90 degrees north and the South Pole is 90 degrees south. When any latitude line is given, it is necessary to tell if it is north or south latitude.

Longitude lines or *meridians* are lines on the globe that run from the North Pole to the South Pole. Each line is the same length. The line which is numbered 0 runs through Greenwich, England. This line is called the *prime meridian*. The other lines tell where locations are west or east of the prime meridian. These lines are numbered from 1 to 180 degrees west and from 1 to 180 degrees east.

Only one line is numbered 180 degrees and it is directly opposite Line 0. This line is called the *date line*. If you are traveling west and cross the date line on Friday, you pass into Saturday. But if you are traveling east on Friday, you go back to Thursday. Look on a globe to see where the date line divides the old day from the new. Remember this line if you're traveling and want to miss a test! Also remember that you must know if a longitude line is east or west of the prime meridian, or you'll get lost.

Longitude and latitude lines are much like the streets in your city. You follow one street until it meets another. On a globe, follow 40 degrees north latitude until it meets 75 degrees west longitude. Where these lines meet you'll find Philadelphia, Pennsylvania.

If your relative lives 20 degrees north and 100 degrees west, would you pack a swimming suit or snowshoes?

What is a Hemisphere?

Do you have a friend or relative who can see both the southern and northern *hemispheres* at the same time?

What's a hemisphere? "Hemi" means "half." So, a hemisphere is half a sphere or half a globe (even though there are four of them).

The equator divides the globe into two equal parts

called the northern and southern hemispheres. The northern hemisphere is that half of the globe north of the equator. The southern hemisphere is that half of the globe south of the equator.

The prime meridian and the 180 degree meridian also divide the globe into two equal parts. The half west of the prime meridian and east of the 180 degree meridian is the western hemisphere. The half east of the prime meridian and west of the 180 degree meridian is the eastern hemisphere.

So where can you see both the southern and northern hemispheres? Ecuador—the country named for the equator—is one place. It's the only country in the world where the temperature and latitude reach zero. Quito, the capital, is located almost on the equator and is 9,000 feet above sea level.

In which hemispheres do you and your relatives live? In which hemispheres did your ancestors live?

Oceans To Sail

Look at the globe again and see if you would sail the *ocean* to visit the countries on your list. The ocean covers 71 percent of the earth's surface. It is divided into four separate oceans. They are the Arctic, Atlantic, Pacific, and Indian. The Arctic is mostly covered with ice, so it is different from the others.

Most likely your ancestors sailed the Atlantic or Pacific oceans to come to the United States. These two oceans are divided by the equator into the North and South Pacific, and into the North and South Atlantic. The Pacific is the largest ocean—larger than all the land on earth. The highest waves are here, too. The highest one ever seen was 112 feet tall. The Pacific is also the deepest ocean. In fact, the deepest point on earth—the Mariana Trench—is under the Pacific and reaches 6.8 miles down into the earth near the intersection of 10 degrees north and 140 degrees east. Can you find the trench on a globe?

South of the United States is the Atlantic's deepest point. The Puerto Rico Trench, near the island of Puerto Rico, reaches 5.4 miles under the sea. Look for it near the intersection of 20 degrees north and 70 degrees west.

The world's highest tides—averaging 40 feet between high and low water—surge into the Bay of Fundy between the Canadian provinces of Nova Scotia and New Brunswick. Once the tides reached a record 103 feet at Burntcoat Head in the Minas Basin, Nova Scotia, in 1869. This bay is near 45 degrees north and 65 degrees west.

If your ancestors came from India or Pakistan, they may have sailed the waters of the Indian Ocean. This ocean has the world's greatest source of offshore oil. The Java Trench, 4.5 miles deep, is its deepest point. Look for the trench near the intersection of 10 degrees south and 110 degrees east.

Continents To Travel

To which main land areas, or *continents,* do the countries on your list belong? The continents are: Asia, Europe, Africa, North America, South America, Australia, and Antarctica.

All of the United States except Hawaii is a part of the North America continent. Hawaii is separated from continents by the Pacific Ocean.

The ancestors of most Americans came from the continents of Europe, South America, and Africa. In recent years, many Americans have come from Asia. Select the continent from which your ancestors came and compare it with the North American continent. You also can select the continent that you'd most like to visit and compare it to your own.

Here is some information about the continents. Facts that are world records, such as the longest river in the world, are listed under the heading "World Facts" at the end of each continent's section. The continents are listed according to size.

ASIA

Asia is the largest continent, covering almost one-third of the world's land area.

More than half of the world's people live in Asia.

The dividing line between Asia and Europe runs along the Ural Mountains, through the Caspian and Black Seas and into the Mediterranean. The line continues to divide Asia and Africa by running through the Suez Canal and the Red Sea.

Java, Borneo, Sumatra, and the smaller islands near them are considered a part of "tropical Asia." The island of Cyprus (which is south of the country of Turkey and in the Mediterranean Sea) is a part of Asia, too.

Population: 2,995,000,000 (estimate for mid-1988)*

Size: 17,100,000 square miles*

Climate: All climates are found, as continent stretches from the Arctic to the equator.

Longest River: Yangtze (also called Chang Jiang, meaning "long river"); runs some 3,434 miles from the mountains of Tibet to the Yellow Sea near the port of Shanghai. Almost half of China's crops are grown along its banks.

Highest Waterfall: Falls of Gersoppa, also called Jog Falls; located in a small stream (Sharavati) on the border of northwest Mysore, India. Mysore is an Indian state located in the southern part of the country.*

Largest Desert: Gobi Desert, in Mongolia and People's Republic of China; 500,000 square miles. It is the northernmost of all deserts.

Most Famous Legendary Creature: The Abominable Snowman, or Yeti, is said to live in the Himalayan Mountain range. The Yeti resembles a tall, hairy ape. *See also* "Bigfoot," which is North America's most famous legendary creature. Then ask yourself, "Are Bigfoot and the Abominable the same kind of creature?"

Famous Mysterious Place: Palaces, temples, and a great tower are part of the ruined ancient city of

*Source for continent area figures: *Goodes World Atlas, 13th Edition*. Chicago: Rand McNally and Company, 1970.

*Source for most of the geographical information about the continents: *Webster's New Geographical Dictionary*. Springfield, Massachusetts: G. & C. Merriam Co., Publishers, 1980.

Angkor, which is northwest of Phnom Penh, the capital of Cambodia. Founded in the first century by people from the Union of Myanmar (formerly Burma), the city was abandoned in the 15th century. What happened to the city and why did the people leave?

Man-made Wonder: Do you know that the Great Wall of China is visible from the moon? With walls 12 to 25 feet thick and from 20 to 50 feet high, this gigantic structure winds across the mountains and valleys of the People's Republic of China for 1,500 miles (about the distance from Denver, Colorado, to Washington, D.C.). The wall was built over 2,000 years ago to keep out invaders from the north.

World Facts:

Highest Point: Mount Everest, between Nepal and Tibet; 29,078 feet above sea level

Lowest Point: Shore of the Dead Sea, in Israel/Jordan; 1,302 feet below sea level. Towns on the shore of the Dead Sea, almost 1,300 feet below sea level, are the lowest towns in the world.

Tallest Mountain Range: The Himalayan mountain range; average elevation of 20,000 feet. The range stretches across parts of India, Nepal, Tibet, and the People's Republic of China for 1,500 miles. This mountain range includes Mount Everest.

Largest Saltwater Lake: Caspian Sea between Asia and Europe; 143,550 square miles

Deepest Lake: Lake Baikal or Lake Baykal in Siberia, U.S.S.R.; 5,715 feet deep

Largest Country (by size): Union of Soviet Socialist Republics; 8,649,512 square miles. Its greatest length north and south is about 2,800 miles; its greatest length west and east is about 6,800 miles. The country is more than twice the size of the United States, including Alaska.

Largest Country (by population): People's Republic of China, 1,571,400,000 (estimate for the year 2100)

Largest City (by population): Tokyo-Yokohama, Japan; 29,971,000 (estimate for the year 2000). Yokohama is considered part of the Tokyo urban-industrial region.

AFRICA

Africa is the second largest continent.

Population: 623 million (estimate for mid-1988)

Size: 11,600,000 square miles (includes offshore islands)

Largest Country (by size): Sudan; 967,500 square miles

Largest Country (by population): Nigeria; 508,800,000 (estimate for the year 2100)*

Largest City (by population): Cairo, Egypt; 12.5 million (estimate for the year 2000)**

Highest Point: Mount Kilimanjaro in northeast Tanzania; 19,340 feet above sea level

*World Population in Transition by Thomas W. Merrick. Ann Arbor, Michigan: Population Reference Bureau, Inc., April 1986.
**World Population Profile, 1985, Table 2; US Bureau of the Census, Department of Commerce.

Lowest Point: Lake Assal, in Djibouti; 512 feet below sea level.

Climate: Africa is the hottest continent. Nearly one-third of Africa is desert.

Largest Lake: Lake Victoria in east central Africa; 26,828 square miles

Highest Waterfall: Tugela Falls; drops 3,110 feet in five falls in the Republic of South Africa

Famous Mysterious Place: The Great Pyramid, near Cairo, Egypt. This 5,000-year-old tomb for the Egyptian King Khufu covers 13 acres and originally was 480 feet high. Using only simple tools, the ancient Egyptians managed to move and raise immense slabs of limestone and granite weighing up to 30 tons a piece. Except for the Great Wall of China, the Great Pyramid is the largest single ancient structure.

Scenic Wonder: Victoria Falls on the border of Zambia and Zimbabwe. At a point where the Zambezi River is almost 6,000 feet wide, the water drops into a narrow crack in the earth's surface. A heavy cloud of mist rises up from the base of the falls and the thundering roar of falling water can be heard for miles.

World Facts:

Longest River: The Nile; 4,187 miles from its headwaters near Lake Victoria to the Mediterranean Sea

Largest Desert: The Sahara; 3,500,000 square miles. It sweeps across north Africa from the Atlantic Ocean to the Red Sea. Its elevation ranges from 100 feet below sea level to more than 11,000 feet above sea level.

Greatest Waterfall Flow: Boyoma Falls, Zaire; 600,000 cubic feet per second, average annual flow

NORTH AMERICA

North America is the third largest continent.

Greenland, the largest island in the world (840,000 square miles), is considered a section of North America.

Population: 416 million (estimate for mid-1988)*

Size: 9,400,000 square miles

Largest Country (by size): Canada; 3,851,809 square miles, includes 291,571 square miles of water.

Largest Country (by population): United States; 308,700,000 (estimate for the year 2100)

Largest Cities (by population): Mexico City, Mexico, 28 million; New York City, New York, 15 million; Los Angeles, California, 11 million (all estimates for the year 2000)

Highest Point: Mount McKinley, Alaska; 20,320 feet above sea level

Lowest Point: Death Valley, California; 282 feet below sea level

Climate: All major types of climates can be found. *See* Chapter 6 to learn about climates.

Longest River: Mackenzie River in Canada; 2,600 miles long

*Source for population figures: Population Reference Bureau, Inc.

Most Famous Legendary Creature: Bigfoot, or Sasquatch (an Indian name meaning "wild man of the woods"), in the Rocky Mountains of Canada and the United States. Bigfoot is said to resemble a large, hairy ape.

Famous Mysterious Place: Mystery Hill, New Hampshire. Stone structures that once may have been an observatory date back 4,000 years. Who built the site? What did these people know about the universe?

Scenic Wonder: Imagine that the earth suddenly opens up where you are to expose a beautiful mountain range of changing colors. In northern Arizona there's such a place where the ground falls away and you look down into the largest canyon in the world—the Grand Canyon. The Grand Canyon is 277 miles long, from 600 feet to 18 miles wide, and as much as a mile deep.

World Facts:

Largest Freshwater Lake: Lake Superior; covers some 31,800 square miles and forms a natural boundary between the United States and Canada

Longest Cave: Mammoth Cave in Kentucky; over 150 miles long, on five levels

Highest Surface Wind Speeds Recorded: Mount Washington, New Hampshire. In 1934, winds of 231 miles per hour were recorded. In a tornado at Wichita Falls, Texas, winds of 280 miles per hour were recorded in 1958.

Tallest Skyscraper: Sears Tower, in Chicago, Illinois; 110 stories or 1,454 feet high

Tallest Tower: Canadian National Railroad Tower, Toronto, Canada; 1,822 feet high

Largest Building: Louisiana Superdome in New Orleans, Louisiana; covers 52 acres

Longest Bridge: Lake Ponchartrain Number 2 in New Orleans, Louisiana; 23.87 miles long. The bridge spans Lake Ponchartrain.

Highest Bridge: The Royal Gorge Bridge; 1,053 feet above the Arkansas River in central Colorado

Most Snow in One Year: Mt. Ranier, Washington; 1,125 inches in 1971–72

SOUTH AMERICA

South America is the fourth largest continent.

Population: 286 million (estimate for mid-1988)

Size: 6,800,000 square miles

Largest Country (by size): Brazil; 3,284,426 square miles

Largest Country (by population): Brazil; 293,200,000 (estimate for the year 2100)

Largest City (by population): São Paolo, Brazil; almost 26 million (estimate for the year 2000)

Highest Point: Mount Aconcagua in west Argentina near the Chilean border; 22,834 feet above sea level

Lowest Point: Valdés Peninsula in Argentina, which extends into the Atlantic Ocean; 131 feet below sea level

Climate: Almost all types of climates. Most of South

America is hot, while the high Andes and far south are cool most of the year.

Longest River: Amazon; 4,000 miles; carries more water than any other river in the world

Famous Mysterious Place: Machu Picchu—a beautiful ancient city high in the Andes of Peru—is said to be a ceremonial city where the Inca Indians worshipped. Steep stairways lead to stone shrines, fountains, and palaces. How was the city built, and when? Why was it deserted?

Scenic Wonder: Cotopaxi, a snowcapped volcano, rises 50 miles south of the equator in the Andes of Ecuador. It is among the world's most active volcanoes.

World Facts:

Longest Mountain Range: The Andes. They extend the entire length of South America's west coast, from Cape Horn in the south to Colombia in the north, a distance of 4,500 miles. Many volcanoes and earthquakes are in the mountains.

Highest Capital: La Paz, Bolivia, is 12,001 feet above sea level.

Highest Waterfall: Angel Falls in southeast Venezuela; drops 3,212 feet from a flat-topped mountain

Highest Navigable Lake: Lake Titicaca; 12,500 feet above sea level along the Peru and Bolivian border

ANTARCTICA

Antarctica is the fifth largest continent.

Population: People do not live here permanently.

Size: 5,100,000 square miles (about the size of the United States and Europe combined)

Highest Point: Vinson Massif, Sentinel Range; 16,860 feet

Lowest Point: Unknown

Climate: Antarctica is the coldest continent, although once it was a rain forest. The sun doesn't appear at all from mid-May until the end of July.

Wildlife: Penguins, seals, whales, gulls, petrels, skuas (birds), and tiny wingless insects. Plants include moss, lichens, and two kinds of flowering plants.

World Facts:

Coldest Temperature Recorded:–126.9 degrees Fahrenheit; at Vostock, Antarctica, on August 24, 1960

Thickest Ice: 9,000 feet, in places along the coastal region of Wilkes Land. The ice sheet there is the largest in the world and contains 90 percent of the world's ice.

Largest Iceberg: an Antarctic iceberg, over 12,000 square miles, seen in the South Pacific, 1956. This iceberg was larger than the country of Belgium.

EUROPE

Europe is the sixth largest continent.

Population: 497 million (estimate for mid-1988)*

Size: 3,800,000 square miles*

*Numbers include Iceland, Great Britain, European Russia, and Turkey.

Largest Country (by size): France; 210,038 square miles

Largest Country (by population): West Germany; 61 million (estimate for year 2100)

Largest City (by population): Paris, France; about 9 million (estimate for the year 2000)

Highest Point: Mount El'brus in the Caucasus Mountains, west of the Black Sea; 18,481 feet

Lowest Point: Caspian Sea; about 92 feet below sea level

Climate: All major types of climates, except tropical climates and deserts.

Longest River: The Volga flows northwest of Moscow to the Caspian Sea; 2,293 miles long

Largest Lake: Lake Ladoga, U.S.S.R.; 6,835 square miles

Most Famous Legendary Creature: "Nessie"—the dinosaur-like water beast with a long thin neck and small head—is said to live in Loch Ness, a lake in northern Scotland.

Famous Mysterious Place: Stonehenge—a ring of gigantic stones set in place by a mysterious people 4,500 years ago—is in southern England. Did the stones form a calendar, observatory, temple, or all three?

Scenic Wonder: Imagine mountains sloping steeply down to valleys full of deep blue water inlets called fjords. Fjords in Norway were formed when glaciers carved out the valleys and then were flooded by the sea.

World Facts:

Largest Ice Cave: Eisriesenwelt (a German word meaning "giant ice world") Cave; reaches 25 miles into the Alps south of Salzburg, Austria

Smallest Country By Population and Area: Vatican City, located within the city of Rome, Italy; .2 square miles; population, 1,000

Longest Bridge Span: Humber Estuary, Hull, England; 4,626 feet.

Longest-Lasting Rainbow: Wales, over three hours, August 14, 1979

AUSTRALIA

Australia is the world's smallest continent.

It is the lowest continent, as one half (the Western Plateau) is only 1,000 feet above sea level.

It is the only continent made up of one country, Australia.

Population: 26,000,000 (estimate for mid-1988)

Size: 2,900,000 square miles

Largest City: Sydney; 3,472,700 (population estimate for mid-1988). Sydney covers 670 square miles.

Highest Point: Mount Kosciusko; 7,316 feet above sea level

Lowest Point: Lake Eyre; 52 feet below sea level. Lake Eyre is also the largest salt lake in Australia, covering 3,600 square miles.

Climate: Australia is the driest continent. It is mostly desert and has many salt lakes. No active volcanoes are on the continent.

Longest River: The Murray (1,609 miles) and Darling (1,702 miles) river system.

Most Mysterious Place and Scenic Wonder: Ayers Rock—a gigantic red sandstone rising 1,143 feet above the Australian desert—changes colors. It is rose at dawn, bright orange during the day, blood-red at sunset, and lavender at dusk. Artwork on cave walls in the rock's base show subjects sacred to the Aboriginals—Australia's earliest inhabitants.

World Facts:

Longest Reef: Great Barrier Reef off Queensland, northeastern Australia; 1,200 miles long

Highest Waterspout: Sighted off Eden, NSW, Australia; 5,014 feet high with a diameter of ten feet, on May 16, 1898.

Deepest Submarine Canyon: 25 miles south of Esperance, western Australia; 6,000 feet deep and 20 miles wide

Largest Rock Pinnacle: Lord Howe Island, off southeast coast of Australia; 1,843 feet high

Conflicting and Changing Facts

Facts and information about the continents often disagree. For example, one reference book says that Mount Aconcagua, the highest point in South America, is 23,034 feet above sea level. Another book says its elevation is 22,834 feet, and still another says 22,500. Whenever you find conflicting facts, it's best to ask a librarian or a teacher of geography which reference book is the best source.

51

In the process of searching for facts, check the book's copyright date. This date gives the year the book was published. A book published in 1990 probably has more accurate geographical information than a book published in 1950.

Facts also change because people develop better measuring instruments. A United States satellite first measured a mountain in Pakistan as being taller than Mount Everest. Then new satellite measurements put Everest at 29,078 feet and the other mountain at 28,238 feet.

Keep your eyes and ears open for news in newspapers and on the TV and radio that changes world facts, figures, and even the names of cities and countries. Sears Tower in Chicago, for example, is the world's tallest building. But plans are being made to build a taller building in Chicago. In a few years, Sears Tower may only be the second tallest building in the world.

Remember, too, that population figures change constantly. Countries do not take a *census*, or a count of the population, in the same year. The United States, for example, takes a count of its entire population every ten years, while some other countries take a count every five years. State and city censuses usually are taken during the years between the country's count of its entire population. Thus, country and city population figures or estimates are not for the same year.

The names of countries and cities often change with changes in political power. Burma's name was changed in June 1989 by its military dictatorship to the Union of Myanmar. And its capital, Rangoon, is now Yangon.

Here are some other name changes:

Old Name	New Name
Saigon, Vietnam	Ho Chi Minh City
Peking, China	Beijing
Szechwan, China	Sichuan
Angora, the capital of Turkey	Ankara
Ceylon, an island off the coast of India	Sri Lanka
Nyasaland, Africa	Malawi
South-West Africa	Namibia
Southern Rhodesia, Africa	Zimbabwe
Northern Rhodesia, Africa	Zambia
Congo, Africa	Zaire
Siam	Thailand

While country and city names change often, some other names never seem to change. Rivers that drain into the Black Sea—the Don, Donets, Dniester, and Dnieper—were named some 3,000 years ago by Iranian-speaking people. Aztec Indians who first came to Mexico about 800 years ago called a beautiful area "Michoacán," which means "Land of Fishermen." Today this same land is the Mexican state of Michoacán.

Just For Fun

To find out which geographical places recently have had name changes, check with a reference librarian in a public or state library. Your state library is located in your state capital. Ask for booklets titled "Decisions on Geographical Names in the United States." These booklets, available from the U.S. Board on Geographic Names, give up-to-date information on United States name changes. The Board also publishes booklets on world name changes.

Just For Fun Create A Special-Interest Grid

The grid that follows is an example of what you can do with the information about continents. You can fill in some of the blanks on the grid by reading this book and by doing some research in the library.

You also can create your own special-interest grid. Mysterious places, volcanoes, geysers, famous vacation resorts, and main languages might be some of your headings. Your grid will offer you many chances to learn more about geography.

	CLIMATE	LEGENDARY CREATURES	CAVES	RIVERS
ASIA		Abominable Snowman, or Yeti, is said to live in Himalayan Mountains.		
AFRICA				
NORTH AMERICA				
SOUTH AMERICA				Longest river, Amazon; 4,000 miles.
ANTARCTICA				
EUROPE				
AUSTRALIA	Dry climate. Most interior is desert or near-desert			

★ 4 ★

FROM WHERE DO YOUR PETS AND OTHER ANIMALS COME?

Discovering the history of your pet can lead to interesting places and fascinating stories. For example, Saint Bernard dogs became famous for their rescue work in the early 1800s at Great Saint Bernard Pass in the mountains of Switzerland. Barry, one of the most famous rescue dogs in history, rescued forty semifrozen people from heavy snows.

Some maps show the Hospice du Grand Saint Bernard, which was the shelter where Barry lived and worked. Barry and other Saint Bernards were trained by monks who had devoted themselves to saving the lives of travelers forced to cross the pass each year on foot. In 1800, for example, the dogs were set out to rescue Napoleon's soldiers who were perishing in the snow while attempting to drag themselves over the steep mountain cliffs. The Hospice is one of the highest human habitations in Europe. If you have a Saint Bernard, your dog would enjoy the heavy snows and winters of Great Saint Bernard Pass.

Just For Fun

Where can you find interesting stories like the one about Saint Bernards? Go to the library and look for books about pets and animals. You also can purchase books about pets in local pet shops and bookstores. Once you discover your pet's history, you can search in books about foreign countries for more information about the places from where your pet came.

You also can make a map to explain the places mentioned in your pet's history. You'll want to add words and symbols to the map to tell the story better. Explain your symbols in a key. Put a drawing or a photograph of your pet in the location where it lives now. Add your pet's name, birth date, birthplace, and the names of any other places where it has lived. If you and your pet move, add another place name. Use your imagination, details, and colors to make a creative map about your pet.

Pet Names

Just the name of your pet can lead you to a foreign country, city, or island. The Great Dane, for example, was named for the country of Denmark. Yugoslavia's Dalmatian Coast gave its name to the white dog with a lot of black spots, the Dalmatian. The Angora cat was named after the capital city of Turkey. Angora, however, is now known as Ankara.

Your pet canary is descended from the wild canaries of the Canary Islands, which are in the Atlantic near Africa's northwest coast. But the islands weren't named for these birds. They were named for the wild dogs that once roamed the islands. "Canary" is from the Roman word *canis,* meaning "dog." Thus, the island name means "islands of dogs."

Learn about the places from where your pets or favorite animals originally came. Collect pictures of these places. Look at brochures, magazines, the travel sections of newspapers, and travel agents' advertisements for information. You might want to make a poster or scrapbook with your pictures. Add pictures of your pet or favorite animal. Write about the animal and include this writing with your pictures.

Just For Fun on Zoo Animals

Lions, tigers, and bears are among the thousands of animals that live in zoos. When you visit a zoo, select your favorite animal and do some research in the library to learn about the place from where it came. Most zoos have signs on the animal's cage or habitat area which give the animal's name and the name of the place where it naturally lives. Many zoos try to duplicate the animal's home area. This will give you an idea of the geographical features of the animal's natural surroundings. Perhaps your favorite zoo animal lives in a tropical rain forest, in the arctic cold, or in the African grasslands called savannas.

Zoos, safaris, and park preserves often are the only places where *endangered* animals can safely live. "Endangered" means that the animal is in danger of no longer existing. The Asian elephant, for example, and the larger African elephant once roamed in great herds over all the continents except Australia. Today the Asian elephant lives in the forested areas of some parts of Asia, while the African elephant lives in the central and eastern forests of Africa. People have threatened the elephant's existence by hunting, by polluting, and by destroying the animal's natural living space for man's own use.

Animals That Know Where They Are

Imagine that you are blindfolded and riding on a boat in the Atlantic Ocean. The boat is pitching up and down in the waves and changing directions as it heads out to sea. It's night, so you can't feel the heat of the sun on one side of your face. Music is playing over the loudspeakers to mask the sounds of waves breaking on nearby islands. Can you tell the captain the direction and the distance back to your home port?

You can't, but animals such as whales, birds, and fish would be able to find the way. These creatures are *migratory animals*. They are born with remarkable abilities to find their ways to certain feeding areas in the fall, and then to return to the places where they were born in the spring. The distances between these places may be thousands of miles. Your captain would gladly trade his sea charts, distance measuring instruments, and all his knowledge of geography for such abilities.

Just For Fun

Pick out your favorite migratory animal and make a map of its migration route. Perhaps your favorite is the humpback whale. If you live in Hawaii, you probably have seen humpbacks in the warm-water areas around the islands. They migrated from the Bering and Chukchi seas, moved along the North American coastline, and then swam west to Hawaii.

Or perhaps you have seen humpbacks along the eastern United States coastline from the deck of a whale watching vessel. These humpbacks migrate from south of Greenland, through the Atlantic Ocean, to Bermuda and the West Indies. Where are all these places? If you need help, ask your librarian for special maps that show the migration routes of different animals.

Birds That Follow Routes

In the fall and spring, you've probably heard the deep-throated honking of Canada geese as they stream out in V-formations across the sky. Or maybe you've been to a lake and have seen thousands of long black necks with white cheeks lifted above brown bodies. These birds migrate between their winter feeding grounds and spring breeding areas. Different groups of these geese use different *migration corridors*. One group spends the summer in the Hudson Bay area of Canada. Each fall, the flock rises to fly southwest to Manitoba, and then swings south to pass over western Minnesota and eastern North and South Dakota. Many geese come down to feed and rest at Minnesota's Lac qui Parle Refuge on the upper Minnesota River. Then they go on their way southeast to Swan Lake in north central Missouri, where they spend the winter. Only a few leave Swan Lake and fly into Arkansas and Louisiana. In the spring, the geese follow the same route back to Hudson Bay.

Just For Fun

You can find out when Canada geese and other migrating birds are in your area by asking for information about these animals from your state museum or local nature center and Audubon Society. Your state museum or members of the American Birding Association have "rare bird alert" telephone numbers that you can call to find out which birds are in your area and where they have been seen. A list of "rare bird alert" numbers is available for a fee from the American Birding Association, P.O. Box 6599, Colorado Springs, Colorado 80934.

★ 5 ★

WHERE ARE THE PLACES IN STORYBOOKS?

Did you ever wish you lived on a mountain and had goats? Daisy Hardyment of Oxford, England, wished she did. She was in the middle of reading *Heidi* by Johanna Spyri when she asked her mother, "Is there really a place called Maienfeld?" Her question launched an adventure. Daisy, her mother, and three sisters set off to find Maienfeld and the other places in their favorite stories. They traveled through six countries in Europe searching for Heidi's mountain, Pinocchio's home, and fairy-tale castles. They found Heidi's Alp in Maienfeld, Switzerland, on the Liechtenstein border. In Collodi, Italy, they discovered the settings in *The Adventures of Pinocchio*.

*Author's Note: *Heidi's Alp, One Family's Search for Storybook Europe* by Christina Hardyment is published by the Atlantic Monthly Press, 1987. This adult, nonfiction book contains a bibliography and addresses to the storybook places found in Europe.

A map of West Germany's Fairytale Road—from Bremen to Schwalmstadt—led them to the castles in *Cinderella* and *Rapunzel*, and to the fairytale settings of *Hansel and Gretel, Snow-White,* and *Little Red Riding Hood*. And in the state of Bavaria, on the border between West Germany and Austria, they explored the spectacular castle in *Chitty-Chitty-Bang-Bang*.

Just For Fun

You, too, can begin your own storybook adventure by searching for the places in your favorite books. Perhaps you'd like to find the barn where Wilbur the pig and Charlotte the spider lived in *Charlotte's Web*.

To find it, write down the name of the person who wrote *Charlotte's Web*—E. B. White—and go to the library to seek out reference books about authors. Search in the library's reference section for a set of books titled *Something About the Author*. These volumes are published by Gale Research Incorporated, Detroit, Michigan. Find the index to the volumes and look up the author's name—White, E(lwyn) B(rooks). The numbers after his name will direct you to the volumes that will tell you about his life. Read all of this information and keep a sharp eye out for references made to *Charlotte's Web*. Soon you'll discover that the barn is a real place.

E. B. White wrote all his books on his farm in North Brooklin, Maine, a small town south of Blue Hill on the coast of Blue Hill Bay. He says that he was on his way to the barn to feed his pig when he began to feel sorry for the pig because it was doomed to die. This thought made him so sad that he began to think of ways to save the pig. About the same time, he was watching a big, gray spider and was impressed by how clever she was at weaving. So he worked the spider into his story about the pig.

Something About the Author also will lead you to the many places in the Nancy Drew mystery books. Did you know that "Carolyn Keene" is a name for several people who wrote the Nancy Drew books? The name "Carolyn Keene," however, is in the index and the information there will direct you to Harriet S. Adams, who wrote many of the Nancy Drew mysteries. Her books contain exaggerated versions of happenings in her own childhood and teenage years. She made many trips through the United States, Canada, Mexico, South America, Europe, Asia, and Africa. Many of her Nancy Drew mysteries are set in these places.

Perhaps one of your favorite stories is set in a place you know exists. *Harriet the Spy*—a book by Louise Fitzhugh—takes place in Manhattan. You know Manhattan is a real place because you've heard and read that it's somewhere in New York. A road map showing this state will help you find Manhattan, an island between the Hudson and East Rivers. If you live in Manhattan, or when you visit, can you follow Harriet on her spy route? You'll need a city map of the island to find all the places Harriet goes.

Some places in storybooks, of course, are imaginary. The land of Oz in L. Frank Baum's *The Wizard of Oz* is not a real place. The author says that while he was thinking about a title for the book, he saw the label lettered O-Z on the last drawer of his letter filing cabinet. So he gave the name "Oz" to his fantasy land.

If you can't find your author's name in a reference book about authors, then search the library for books about the author's life and writings. One book—*Writers in Residence, American Writers at Home*, by Glynne Robinson Betts—takes you on a journey into the homes of the people who wrote *Little Women*, *Where the Wild Things Are* and *The Legend of Sleepy Hollow*. By reading this book, you'll find clues to where several storybook places are located. One will lead you to the foot of the Catskill Mountains in New York where Rip Van Winkle slept.

You also might try the *Biography Index*, which tells you where to find information on the lives of famous people. Another source is the *Dictionary of American Biography*, which contains articles on famous Americans. *Who's Who* or *Contemporary Authors* also gives facts about writers who are currently living. *Twentieth Century Authors* gives information on authors who are both living and dead.

Just For Fun

You also can write the author a letter; but find out first if he or she is alive. You can ask if the places in the author's story are real or imaginary. Ask the author, too, where the real places are located. Mail your letter to the publisher of the book. Most publishers will forward letters to authors.

Once you know where the places in your favorite stories are located, make a map showing these places. How far are they from your home and how would you get there? It may take a lot of planning to visit all of your favorite places, especially if you want to find Sleeping Beauty's castle in Sababurg, West Germany, or the setting for the book *Hans Brinker and the Silver Skates* in Holland. But think of all the fun you'll have planning your storybook adventure.

★ 6 ★

WHAT KIND OF A PLACE IS THAT?

What faraway part of the world is most like your home? If you've traveled to other places, you probably have some ideas about how your home compares to the places you've visited. But if you haven't traveled much, it might be fun to do some research to discover the differences and similarities of other parts of the world to your home. Once you find a place that reminds you of your home, read books about it to learn more about its land and people.

Just For Fun

If you can't seem to find a place to compare to your home, locate the latitude on the globe that is closest to your home. Follow this latitude completely around the globe. Which countries and cities does the latitude line cross? Make a list of these places.

Since latitude influences weather, places along your

latitude line may have the same weather you do. Land elevation and the nearness to large bodies of water also are factors in determining the weather. Write down the land elevations for each place on your list. Write down how close the large water areas are. Compare this information to the facts you already have about your home. Now you should have a good idea which country or city is most like the place where you live.

The state of Wyoming, for example, is on the same latitude as the country of Mongolia. Wyoming also lies near 110 degrees west, while the center of Mongolia is 110 degrees east. Wyoming, with its rugged mountains, hills, and grassy plains, looks much like Mongolia. Annual temperatures, precipitations, and land elevations aren't that much different. There are even Mongolian and Wyoming cowboys. And the yellow-skinned Mongol race includes both the people of Mongolia and the American Indians of Wyoming. Yet, Mongolia is different in a lot of ways. The country is about the size of Alaska and its population is two million. Wyoming, the ninth largest state, ranks last in state population—only 490,000 people live there. The main religion of Mongolia is Buddhism and its official language is Mongolian. Mongolia's dry land in the south is a part of one of the world's largest deserts—the Gobi Desert. Books about the history and culture of Mongolia make this faraway country seem very distant, indeed.

Pen Pals

Another way to discover how your hometown compares to other places is to become a pen pal. A pen pal is a person who writes letters to another person who usually lives far away. Friendships started through pen pal letters can continue for years, even though the pen pals are separated geographically and culturally. Some pen pals even visit one another after corresponding for a long time.

Just For Fun

Here are some ways to find a pen pal:

1. Ask your teacher or school librarian to use the *Junior Pen Pals Directory* to establish a classroom exchange of letters with pupils in a classroom of another school. *Junior Pen Pals Directory* lists the names and addresses of principals, teachers, and other educators who are interested in helping young people find pen pals. The *Directory* covers all 50 states, Washington, D.C., Puerto Rico, and the Virgin Islands. Your school and local public library should have a copy of the *Directory*. You can also obtain a copy by writing to Laidlaw Brothers, 8020 West Madison Street, River Forest, Illinois 60305-5565.

2. You can pick a pen pal from the United States, Canada, or another foreign country by writing to the Student Letter Exchange, 630 Third Avenue, New York, New York 10017.

3. You also can find a pen pal from a foreign country by writing to the International Friendship League, 55 Mount Vernon Street, Boston, Massachusetts 02108, or by writing to World Pen Pals, 1690 Como Avenue, St. Paul, Minnesota 55108.

Writing to Your Pen Pal

Here are some things that you might want to include in your first pen pal letter:

—Your name, nickname, birthdate, birthplace, school, and grade.

—A description of yourself. How tall are you? What is your hair and eye color? Include a small picture of yourself if you have one.

—A description of your family. List the names of your family members. Give the ages of your brothers and sisters.

—Your interests and hobbies.

—A description of your hometown. Take a picture or make a photocopy of the map you made of your town and send it to your pen pal.

—Here are some questions you can ask your pen pal: What are the names of your family members? What are the ages of your brothers and sisters? What jobs do you and your parents have? Do you have any pets? What are your hobbies and interests? What did you eat for breakfast? What happened in school today? What do you like best about school? What interesting things are there to do in your town? What is the weather like during the year?

Questions such as these will help you to learn more about your pen pal and the place where he or she lives.

Here is an example of a pen pal letter from San Diego, California:

Hi Susan,

How are you? I'm fine. Sorry, but this pen isn't working too great. Well, my name is Sally Stevenson. I'm 12 years old. My birthday is July 6 and I'm in the sixth grade. I guess you could say I'm sort of boy crazy. I have light brown hair about eight inches past my shoulders. I have hazel eyes, a few freckles, and a little scar on my chin from a dog bite I got when I was three. I have a sister Sara who is nine. My mom is named Sally, too. My dad's name is Sam. We have a dog named Sharon and a cat named Checkers. We also have a parakeet named Angelo. He can say 40 words. I'm sorry, but it would take too long to write them all.

We are supposed to be getting a male golden retriever puppy. I will keep him for 13 months. You see, I'm in a club called 4-H. That's where you raise animals or do art or gardening or leather craft. We are going to raise this puppy to be a guide dog for the blind. I can hardly wait.

My hobbies are swimming, keeping fit, horseback riding (I don't have a horse), and collecting unicorn things. I love unicorns! I'm sorry, but I can't explain where San Diego is in California. When my dad was little he lived in a little town called Bowling Green. That was in Indiana.

Well, next time you write please tell me about your family and your hobbies. Thanks for writing to me. Now I have to go. Bye.

Yours truly,
Sally Stevenson

Please write soon.

Mystery Towns

Since pen pals often exchange small gifts and birthday cards, you can create a mystery box for your pen pal. Select a town or city in your country or state and learn all you can about it. Then put clues that will identify this place inside a small box and mail the box to your pen pal. It's more fun, of course, if your pen pal also mails you a mystery box containing clues to a town in his or her state or country. Then you can compete with your pen pal to see who is the first to identify the mystery town.

Suppose you picked Sherwood, Oregon, a small town south of Portland. Here are some clues you could include:

- A map of the Columbia River.
- Ash from Mount St. Helens. This volcano erupted in 1986.
- A picture of a beaver. Oregon's nickname is "the beaver state."
- A copy of headlines from the community's newspaper.
- A branch from a Douglas fir, Oregon's state tree.

Digging a Hole to China

Does your home resemble the place directly opposite you on the globe? Some people believe they are opposite China because they've heard the expression that if you dig a hole deep enough, you'll end up in China. Last summer, Kathy spent two weeks digging a hole to China in her backyard with a spoon, while her friend Sean used a shovel and dug such a big hole that his mother fell into it when she came home from work.

Of course, you can't dig a hole straight through the earth. But you can discover where your hole would end. Here's how you can find out:

Just For Fun

1. Locate your town's latitude and longitude on the globe or world map. Whatever your latitude is, change its direction to the opposite. If you live at 40 degrees north, for example, change the latitude to 40 degrees south.

2. Write down the number of your longitude line. Subtract this number from 180, then change the direction of that difference. For example, if your longitude is 89 degrees west, then subtract 89 from 180. The difference is 91. Now change the direction. Your opposite longitude is 91 degrees east.

The person living near the intersection of 40 degrees north and 89 degrees west is on the opposite side of the world from the Indian Ocean. This person's hole would end in the sea. If you live in Hawaii, the opposite side of the world is the Kalahari Desert in southern Africa.

What happened to China? If you want to dig to China, you had better write a relative or get a pen pal in Chile or Argentina and ask that person to start digging for you.

Where are Chile and Argentina? If you don't know, look up the names in an encyclopedia or in the table of contents or index of a book of maps. Then locate these countries on a world map or globe.

★ 7 ★

WHERE'S THE PERFECT PLACE?

If you could live anywhere in the world, where would it be? Is it a place where life is easy and where there aren't any problems and schoolwork? A place where everyone likes you and where you never want to leave?

You have probably dreamed of or imagined a perfect place. Can you find your place in the real world? Let's say that you're a baseball fan, so your dream is to see a lot of baseball teams during your spring break. Florida could be your special place, since most of the teams go there for spring training.

Or maybe you like to fish and camp. Head for Canada, which has more lakes and rivers than any other country in the world. It also has the world's longest coastline—56,453 miles of waterfront. Or perhaps you'd like to go somewhere where fat is beautiful. You'll be excited to know that boys like heavy girls in the Kingdom of Tongo. Where's Tongo? Look 20 degrees south by the date line.

Or maybe weather really affects you. Are you one of those people who can't stand the cold or tornadoes? Would you prefer to live in a place where there's only one season? Or do you like all four seasons—fall, winter, spring, and summer?

To find your perfect place, make a list of what you like and dislike. Your list might look something like this:

Hobbies
shell and rock collecting

Interests
dinosaurs

Don't Like:
winter and ice
pollution

Do Like:
amusement parks
exploring new places

Let's take each item on this list and match it to a real geographical place.

Amusement Parks

Perhaps you've been to the world's largest amusement park, Walt Disney World near Orlando, Florida. It's 43 square miles, an area twice the size of Manhattan Island in New York. Not only do you need a road map to get there, but you also need a map of the parking lot so you can find your car when you're ready to leave. Get a map of the park, too, or you'll spend most of your time at Cinderella Castle, the place where most lost people are finally found.

80

Walt Disney World is a good place to learn about other countries. EPCOT (Experimental Prototype Community of Tomorrow) Center, which is a part of the park, has a World Showcase area presenting the social and cultural heritages of almost a dozen countries. Each country is represented by famous landmarks and street scenes familiar to world travelers. The countries represented are: Mexico, Canada, the United States, Norway, Germany, Italy, France, Morocco, the United Kingdom, Japan, and the People's Republic of China.

Just For Fun

How far is Disney World from your home? Get out a road atlas of the United States and find out. Look for United States mileage charts. Orlando will be listed along one side of the chart. Your city or a city close to it will be listed along the other side of the chart. Follow the Orlando column to where it comes together with your city's column. The number where the two columns intersect is the number of miles from your city to Orlando.

If Orlando seems too far from your home, look for other amusement parks that are closer. Perhaps Disneyland in Anaheim, California, is closer. Six Flags' Great Adventure in Jackson, New Jersey, is halfway between Philadelphia, Pennsylvania, and New York City. No other park outside Africa has as many wild animals. You can see these animals from your car window as you drive through the park.

Exploring New Places and Shell and Rock Collecting

What better place to go exploring and shell and rock collecting than on an island? The United States has over 26,000 islands. Of these, Alaska has 5,668. One of Alaska's islands, Little Diomede, helps to mark the boundary line between Alaska and the Union of Soviet Socialist Republics (U.S.S.R.). The line runs between Little Diomede and the U.S.S.R.'s Big Diomede. The islands are only two miles apart.

As you know, Hawaii is an island state. Hawaii's islands, of which there are eight main ones, stretch out for 1,600 miles. Honolulu, the capital, is on the island of Oahu. The city has a daily winter temperature of about 81 degrees Fahrenheit, so it doesn't snow there.

Here are some other adventurous islands for you to explore. Can you discover where they are and how far away they are from your home?

St. Helena—Napoleon, whose soldiers the Saint Bernards saved, was sent into exile here in 1815 by the English. His house still stands today. Look for the island near the center of the mid-Atlantic Ocean between Africa and South America.

Easter Island—If you like mysteries, you'll want to learn all you can about this volcanic island. It belongs to Chile in South America, although it is located 2,300 miles west of there. Hundreds of tall stone statues stand near the shore, facing inland. Who made them and why?

82

British West Indies—Blackbeard, Captain Kidd, and other pirates hid in the coves of these islands. Perhaps a treasure or two awaits you if you can manage to explore Dead Chest and Gallows Cay. You'll have fun finding these places among the several West Indies possessed by the United Kingdom of Great Britain and Northern Ireland. The islands include the Cayman Islands, Montserrat, and the Turks and Caicos Islands. Look for them in the Caribbean Sea near Cuba and Puerto Rico.

Isles of Shoals—You'll not have any problems finding this archipelago of nine granite islands about ten miles southeast of Portsmouth, New Hampshire, in the Gulf of Maine. Captain Kidd reportedly buried treasure there. Blackbeard took his last and fifteenth wife there for their honeymoon and then left her. Her ghost and the ghost of one of Captain Kidd's men supposedly haunt the islands. Today, Shoals is noted for its summer field station dedicated to the study of the marine sciences.

Galapagos Islands—Four-eyed fish, yard-long lizards, sunflower trees, and tortoises with shells as large as bathtubs live on the Galapagos Islands, 600 miles off the coast of Ecuador in the Pacific Ocean. The unusual plants and animals on the islands inspired Charles Darwin to create his theory of evolution—the idea that early, simpler forms of plants and animals have changed over a long period of time into the many different plants and animals living today.

The islands are named after the giant tortoises. *Galapago* is an old Spanish name for "tortoise."

Dinosaur Places

Are there any dinosaur parks near your home? You can see thousands of dinosaur tracks at Dinosaur State Park in Wethersfield, Connecticut, south of Hartford. Dinosaurs roamed this area 200 million years ago. To see places where dinosaurs died and the remains of their bodies, head for Dinosaur National Monument in northwestern Colorado and northeastern Utah. Dinosaurs of almost every size once lived in this area.

More than 30 kinds of dinosaurs have been unearthed in Dinosaur Provincial Park, which is east of Calgary in Alberta, Canada. Dinosaur remains have been found on every continent. Canada has more dinosaur bones than any other country.

If you visit the Page Museum at La Brea Tar Pits in Los Angeles you can see life-size models of mammoths stuck in a real tar pit. Hundreds of skeletons of mammoths, saber-tooth tigers, and other prehistoric animals have been found in the tar pits here.

A museum near your home may have dinosaur skeletons displayed in lifelike poses. The Field Museum of Natural History in Chicago—one of the largest natural history museums in the world—has four dinosaurs on display.

Cold and Hot Places

Do you live in an area where winter storms and hot, humid summers are common? The kind of weather you have during the year is called your *climate*.

The earth is divided into wide climate *zones*. These

zones exist because of the angle at which the sun's rays strike the earth. The farther you are from the equator, the more slanted the sun's rays are. The slanted rays can't warm up the earth as much as the direct rays.

The direct rays, which are the warmest, reach 23½ degrees north and 23½ degrees south of the equator. Lines on a globe mark the zone. The northern line is called the *Tropic of Cancer;* the southern line is the *Tropic of Capricorn.* The zone between these lines is known as the *tropical zone.* Tropical climates are the warmest on earth. Frequent thunderstorms lasting only a short time keep the area very wet. There's only one season—summer. Plants grow all year, and the leaves of trees don't change colors in the fall. If you live in Honolulu, Hawaii, you're in the tropical zone.

North and south of the tropical zones are two *subtropicalzones.* The very southern part of the United States is in the subtropical zone that lies north of the equator. There are seasons here, but the winters are very mild and it hardly ever snows. At 30 degrees north and south latitude are most of the world's deserts, usually located on the west sides of continents.

North and south of the subtropics are the *middle latitude zones.* Here the summers can be very hot, and the winters are long with a lot of snow and ice. Most of the world's people live in these zones.

The *polar zones* are the coldest. Snow and ice cover the ground most of the year. Summers aren't warm enough for any agricultural products to grow. And, as you may have guessed, not many people live here.

The polar zones are divided by imaginary lines on the globe. The *Arctic Circle* marks the northern zone at 66½ degrees north and the *Antarctic Circle* marks the southern zone at 66½ degrees south. Northern Alaska lies within the Arctic Circle.

Polluted Places

Is there a place in the world that isn't polluted? You can discover what some of the pollutants are in the world by reading your local newspaper and by listening to the news on radio and television. Stories about pollution killing animals and plants, and poisoning the soil, water, and air are in the news every day. Unfortunately, pollution is all over the world.

Everyone in your community is affected by pollution. To find out how pollution affects you, ask yourself these questions:

Was your school ever closed so that the cancer-causing building material asbestos could be removed? Have the drinking fountains in your school ever been turned off because the water was contaminated with lead? Has your school cafeteria ever refused to serve certain foods because of the poisonous insecticides used on them? Has your school or home been tested for radon, a cancer-causing, odorless gas? Has a beach near your home been closed because it was polluted with human wastes or with materials from hospital surgical rooms? Have you ever found a dead animal with a fishnet or plastic bag around its head? Does the air in your community smell like rotten eggs, soybeans, or smoke? Do you swim in polluted water?

If you've answered "yes" to any of these questions,

then you have identified a pollution problem that affects you. Compare your problem or any others that you know your community has to some of these world-wide sad facts about pollution:

Brazil—Birds do not live along the four rivers flowing near São Paulo in eastern Brazil. São Paulo is South America's largest city and has more skyscrapers than Chicago. Cubatao, an industrial and chemical manufacturing center near the city, releases tons of noxious gases into the air each day. As a result, the trees near the complex are dead. Living creatures don't live in the soil. Cubatao is called the "valley of death." Look for São Paulo where the Tropic of Capricorn crosses 50 degrees west.

Japan—Many of this country's lakes are turning green and red because tiny plants called algae are feeding on the phosphates from detergents dumped there. Japan and the United States are among the most polluted countries in the world.

West Germany and Switzerland—Acid rain is killing the forests of these two countries. Acid rain is formed from nitrogen oxides produced by cars and power stations. It's also formed when coal and oil containing sulfur is burned and produces sulfur dioxide. This mixes with rain to produce an acid that injures needles and leaves while changing the chemistry of the soils. Acid rain also pollutes water areas and slowly washes away the outsides of buildings and monuments.

Union of Soviet Socialist Republics (U.S.S.R.)—An explosion in a nuclear power plant at Chernobyl in 1986 spread radioactive materials over a large area. The resulting cloud of radiation killed many people and animals. Crops had to be destroyed and the topsoil removed because they were contaminated. You probably won't find this 800-year-old city on a world map, but it is in the Ukraine, which is the main wheat producing region of the U.S.S.R. The name "Chernobyl" means "Wormwood," the Biblical name given the great star in the book of Revelation that fell from heaven "burning as it were a lamp." The star poisoned one-third of the earth's waters, "and many men died of the waters, because they were bitter."

Does the Perfect Place Exist?

Now that you have matched geographical places to the list of "likes" and "dislikes," can you tell where this person would like to live? What about Hawaii? In Hawaii you can collect shells and rocks, explore new places, and never freeze because there isn't any winter. But would you see Walt Disney World and the remains of dinosaurs?

Just For Fun

For fun, ask your parents to list "likes" and "dislikes," and then try to figure out where they'd like to live. Maybe they'd enjoy a place where there's free health care, high salaries, no income tax, and inexpensive gasoline. Tell them about Brunei. Where's Brunei? Follow the equator until you come to 115 degrees east. But if your parents don't like steamy heat all year long, then Brunei isn't the place for them.

In your search for the perfect place, you may reach the same conclusion Dorothy did in the movie, *The Wizard of Oz:* "There's no place like home."

Where was Dorothy's home?

Kansas, right?

Where would Dorothy be if she didn't know where Kansas was?

The same place you'll be if you don't know where you are.

Lost.

But since you're on your way to learning more geography, you can find Kansas and any other place you want on a place-finding adventure.

Glossary

Archipelago—a group of islands clustered together in the ocean.

Canyon—a deep, narrow valley with steep, rocky sides, formed by running water.

Cardinal directions—the four main directions shown on a map. They are north, south, east, and west.

Compass—an instrument used to determine direction.

Continent—one of the seven large land areas on the earth. They are Asia, Africa, North America, South America, Antarctica, Europe, and Australia.

Date line—an imaginary line through the Pacific Ocean roughly running along the 180 degree longitude line. By international agreement, the calendar date changes when you cross the date line. It's a day later (July 4) when you travel west and a day earlier (July 3) when you travel east.

Desert—a dry, often sandy area that receives little or no rain.

Equator—the imaginary line passing through earth's center and halfway between the North and South Poles.

Fjord—a long, narrow inlet of the ocean between tall cliffs.

Geographical center—that part on which the surface of a particular geographical area would balance if the area were all the same thickness.

Geography—the study of places, why they are there, and what kinds of people, plants, animals, climates, minerals, and land and water areas make up these places.

Globe—a map of the earth in the shape of a sphere.

Grid lines—a pattern of horizontal and vertical lines forming squares on a map, used as a reference for locating places.

Headwaters—the beginning of a river.

Hemisphere—either the northern or southern half of the earth as divided by the equator, or the western and eastern half of the earth as divided by the prime and 180 degree meridians.

In-between directions—the directions halfway between the cardinal directions. They are northwest, northeast, southwest, and southeast.

Island—land that is completely surrounded by water.

Lake—a large inland body of fresh or saltwater.

Land elevation—the height of land above the surface of the ocean after all the wave motions have been smoothed out.

Latitude—lines that run east and west on a map.

Legend or key—an explanation of symbols used on a map.

Longitude—lines that run north and south on a map.

Map—a drawing or picture of a particular place.

Mountain—a gigantic mass of rock that rises high above the surrounding land.

Mountain pass—a gap in a mountain range that serves as a pathway across the mountains.

Mountain range—a long, connected chain of mountains.

Ocean—the entire body of saltwater that covers 71 percent of earth's surface.

Orienting—to place a map so that its directions are the same as the directions on the ground.

Physical map—a map showing mostly natural features, such as land elevation.

Pinnacle—a tall, pointed rock.

Prime meridian—the 0 longitude line, used as a reference from which longitude east and west is measured.

Rain forest—a dense tropical forest receiving at least 100 inches of rain each year.

Reef—a ridge of rocks, sand, or coral that rises near the surface of the water.

River—a large and long stream of water emptying into an ocean or other body of water.

River system—a river and all its tributaries. All of the channels, brooks, and streams that carry water to a river are called tributaries.

Submarine—under the sea. A submarine canyon is a deep, steep-sided depression in the ocean floor.

Symbol—a drawing, color, or words used to represent places and features on a map.

Valley—a lowland between mountains or hills.

Volcano—a mountain formed by materials erupting through the earth's crust. These materials include lava, which is hot, melted rock.

Waterfall—a stream that flows over the edge of a cliff.

Waterspout—a tornado over water.

Zone—a wide belt of climate that encircles the earth.

92

INDEX